Christmas at Janey's Bakeshop

By AM LaMonte

Check out my newsletter!

If you'd like to keep up on all the happenings, freebies, and newest books from AM LaMonte, see the back of this book for details...

Chapter One

"My buns!" Janey shouted, the acrid reek of smoke singeing her nostrils. Whirling, she nearly dropped the pan of cookies she carried in mittened hands, and instead set it with a clatter on the vast wooden kneading board that took up most of the room in the bakery's kitchen.

She dashed to the huge, industrial-sized oven that formed the back wall of the place, its inner racks rotating through like an enormous rotisserie. Ordinarily she found its radiant heat comforting, keeping the place so toasty she rarely had to run the heater all winter. Not when it belched out black smoke, however, as it was doing now.

"Oh no," she moaned as she pulled out trays and trays of what had been going to be someone's Christmas rolls. She set the charred remnants on the kneading board one at a time, pulled off her mittens, and put the back of her gloved hand to her brow. She'd taken two dozen special orders for dinner rolls, due for pickup tomorrow morning, bright and early on Christmas Eve. And now all she had to offer were cinders.

It was her first holiday season in her own brick and mortar bakery, and she'd absolutely bitten off more than she could chew.

It had all started as a well-laid plan. For years after culinary school she'd baked out of the small apartment she shared with two friends, selling her carefully-crafted cakes, cookies, and pies at farmers' markets and by special order. That had kept her busy for a good long while as she honed her craft, and earned her enough to pay her third of the rent each month and keep her in decent shoes. What more did a girl need?

"Then you got cocky," she muttered, forcing herself to tip the charred rolls into the trash can, one tray at a time. With a heavy sigh she turned to the shelves for yeast and sugar to begin a new batch.

Despite small setbacks, for the most part, things had gone very well since opening Janey's Bakeshop. She had a customer base in place already due to her years of cottage baking, and had a decent reputation for working with only the best and freshest ingredients. Like any small business owner she'd taken out loans to get started, but customer demand had been steady from the beginning. By the time the leaves began to change for autumn, she'd been hopeful that getting back in the black was in sight.

Like a curse from a hiphop song, however, she was now a victim of her own success. Holidays were one of the best times of year for bakers, but by Thanksgiving she'd discovered how ill-prepared she was to produce on a larger scale than she'd ever done before. She'd always done everything herself, and though she'd hired two very able bakers—Angelica and Dax—she hadn't yet mastered how to deploy them. She struggled to know what to expect from day to day: today it was slow, tomorrow it was a rush. Demand was steady now, but would it last? How many salaries could she afford? She didn't want to overburden her workers, but she didn't want to hire a new person and then have to let them go in January. Corvallis, Oregon wasn't an enormous town, but surely there were limits to its appetite for her sweet blueberry scones?

Like the rest, she'd brought tonight's stress on herself. Dax and Angelica had offered to stay late and help with the special orders. The weather said there was a big storm rolling in, however, and at the time all the rolls were ready to go, and the eighteen cakes she'd also taken on were baked and only needed frosting. So she'd sent them both home. She could pump out twenty dozen rolls in her sleep, couldn't she? With enough caffeine, and Stevie Wonder blasting? She rolled up her sleeves. At least she'd had a coffee machine installed in the spring—that was one business expense she'd never regretted.

Suddenly the front door jingled. Janey cursed. Of course she had forgotten to lock it and turn the *Open* sign to *Closed*.

Taking a deep breath, she stripped off the latex gloves she was wearing and turned off the massive industrial dough mixer that was churning her yeast, water, flour, and salt. She walked toward the entrance, curving around the central brick barricade that blocked the production side of the bakery from the view of those in the front of the store.

"We're closed," she called out, trying to make her voice both cheery and firm. Dealing with customers, so long as they weren't rude or demanding, was actually one of her favorite parts of the job. There were few things she enjoyed discussing so much as sweets. But now she needed to focus. She needed to concentrate. She needed to buckle down, put in what was required, and Get. This. Done.

"Sorry, closed?"

Janey cased the tall man standing at the counter. It was awkward when this happened, customers finding—or forcing—their way in after closing time. Most left when they realized their mistake. Some stayed and insisted on being served, even though things were shut down.

This man didn't seem too much of a threat. He was tall but narrow, his long arms encased in a tweed jacket, a scarf in muted colors wrapped around his neck. And all topped with a mop of curly dark hair. He wore thin wire glasses and a quizzical expression, giving the all-around impression of an overgrown student looking for the train to wizarding school.

Janey made herself nod slowly. Kindly. The smell of burning bread still tingled in her nostrils. "Closed."

"Oh." He looked down as he spoke, and though she was in a hurry, she couldn't help the way her ears pricked up at the elongated single syllable.

"Are you English?"

"I am." His smile was a mixture of acknowledgment, and perhaps faint dread. Did he think she would ask him to pronounce the phrase "water bottle" repeatedly or something? She ought not to have asked. It wasn't her business where he was from, and besides, she was busy.

"Well, I'll have to ask you to come back another time. I open tomorrow at six." Who had decided these ungodly hours? Oh right. It was her. The problem with running your own business was that you never had anyone to blame for anything but yourself.

"Right," he dithered, in charming British fashion. "It's only, the department party is tonight and I've promised to bring something."

Janey sighed. There was always a party tonight, or a dinner, or a last-minute birthday. As much as the dimple that sparkled in his cheek as he waited for her answer—expectant, maybe, that the dimple would be enough—was intriguing, she couldn't just say yes to someone because he was a little bit cute. The door would open to chaos then.

"I'm very sorry," she repeated. "But we're closed."

At that very moment, everything went dark. And it was with a snick—a light sound that nevertheless echoed in Janey's very soul—that she heard the electric automatic locks on the door snap fast.

"Oh no," she murmured. The festive glow of streetlights and particolored Christmas lights had filtered in through her tall glass windows just moments ago, but the only things visible outside now were darkness and swirling snow. Locked in the back baking, Janey hadn't even noticed that the storm had begun.

"What's happened?" The man strode over to the door and attempted to open it, jiggling the handle uselessly in his hand. He turned back, and Janey gestured helplessly at the darkened ceiling. Her only thoughts were on the eighteen unfrosted cakes on the countertop, the unbaked bread dough still in the mixer, and the industrial oven, whose interior rotation would have ceased, its enormous burners rapidly cooling.

"Oh *no*," she repeated, turning and dashing toward the back. The kitchen, without its usual floodlights, was almost entirely dark. Janey cursed silently as she ripped open a drawer, searching for the emergency candles she had never used, but must be there. She faintly remembered buying them, almost a full year ago, and stashing them somewhere. Just in case. She'd never needed them until now.

She dug and dug, reaching deep, until finally her hand met the waxy sides of several long tapers. She pulled them out, along with their holders, and lit them. The flickering light cast the production floor in a dim, warm glow, creating baroque shadows out of the industrial equipment.

"Um, are you all right?"

Janey turned, startled. The man had come around the barrier and into the kitchen.   "Can you put on a hairnet please?" she said automatically, looking up at his mop of curls. They were a chestnut brown, but in the candle light their edges glowed almost red.

"Oh, yes. I suppose."

She fished one out of a box of disposables and handed it to him. He gamely put it on, and she tried not to smile at the way it flattened the curls to his head until he looked like a 1980s lunch lady. Janey herself wore a floppy baker's cap; she always told people she preferred it because it held her own thick, dark blonde hair better. But the truth was the choice was mainly aesthetic.

"I tried the door," he said pleasantly. "Does it have automatic locks?"

"It does," she said through gritted teeth. She had turned to her mixer and was examining the dough in its enormous bowl. She could perhaps finish the kneading by hand. It would take all night to knead, raise, and divide it into rolls, but that went without saying at this point. But would she even be able to bake them, then? What if the whole night passed and the oven didn't come back on?

"I see. And when would you imagine them opening again?"

Janey shrugged, as if it were obvious. "Whenever the lights come back on."

"Ah."

The man's voice seemed positively cheerful, and Janey finally looked up as she hauled the bowl off the stand, toward the kneading board. "Don't you want to call someone? Just to let them know where you are? I'm here all night anyway, but I'm sure we can call someone to come and get you out." She tried not to let him see her frown at the idea of them breaking her locks.

"Well, there's one problem. I left my phone in my car."

"Oh." Janey blinked. "And mine is dead." She was terrible at remembering to plug it in, and had only done so moments before the store closed tonight. The charger it was connected to in the office too, now, would be useless.

She saw the tall, hair-netted man shrug. "It's all right."

She raised her eyebrows. "All right? Getting locked inside a bakery with a stranger the night before Christmas Eve? What about your party?"

"Well…" he put a hand to his head as if he would have run it through his curls, but found only the hairnet and dropped it again. "The department Christmas party isn't exactly my favorite event of the year."

"Must not be, if this is preferable," Janey murmured, and thought she caught a smile on his face. "Make yourself comfortable then, I guess. You can put your coat and scarf in the office." She eyed his extra layers, hoping he wouldn't be shedding hairs and dust on her beloved equipment as he squeezed past her toward where she pointed in the back.

A moment later he reemerged, jacket and scarf gone, white shirtsleeves rolled to the elbows. At least the bakery promised to stay warm, despite the power-outage. The oven had been roaring all day, and the place was well-insulated.

While he was in the back Janey had pulled on her gloves, and was now lifting the enormous blob of dough from the mixer to the board. She loved bread dough. It was like a yeasty-smelling, vaguely warm creature from another planet. It spread fatly when she plopped it down, and she imagined it sprouting tentacled eyes to look at her. She was grateful every day she had bought the biggest kneading board that would fit back here.

"Perhaps there's something I can help with?"

Janey looked up, resolving to stop forgetting there was another person here apart from herself, her burned buns, and the blob of dough on the counter.

"Oh," she said, sizing him up. "Do you have your food handler's license?

He shook his head, looking mystified.

She bit her lip. "You can't really touch any of the food, then."

"Just how many cakes do you have up there?" he asked, and she saw his eyes had wandered to the shelves where her eighteen cakes waited in their crusty, naked glory. Dax had wrapped them in plastic earlier and they sat patiently now, cooled and ready to be robed in frosting. It was a beautiful sight.

"One and a half dozen," she murmured. And all due for pick-up tomorrow morning.

His eyes grew wide, and she saw they were a deep brown. "You're going to frost all of those tonight?"

Janey nodded determinedly. "I can do it."

"Have you done this many before?"

"You ask a lot of questions!" she said in a high-pitched, garbled voice, and he laughed.

"Listen. I understand there are rules about who can do what here. But I'm willing to help. If this isn't an emergency, what is?"

Janey had pulled out her scraper to start dividing the bread dough into loaf size pieces for the first rise. She glowered at him. "You know how much trouble I could get in for that?"

He spread his hands, and made that dimple show in his cheek again. "No one would ever know."

"You'd know," she said grumpily.

He smiled again. "You think I'm going to blackmail you for cake?"

Janey smiled for the first time. "I wouldn't put it past you."

"Mm, right. Trust no one, and all that. I understand the baking business is rife with corruption and double-dealing."

Janey's smile grew. He was teasing her. "Exactly. I've had the mafia looking to acquire my concern for months. Asking for protection money, etc."

He nodded solemnly. "I'm not remotely surprised. This is a tough neighborhood."

Thinking of the small antique and book shops that lined this part of the university district, the coffee shops with their twee little lights and wrought iron terrace chairs, Janey let out a laugh.
"Have you ever kneaded bread?"

"I need bread all the time. Daily, even."

She rolled her eyes. "That's a bridge too far. Who told you that stupid jokes and wordplay are the way to my heart?" She cringed after saying it. Who here had said anything about hearts? This conversation was veering dangerously close to flirtation, and that was something she had absolutely no time for. Besides being very busy tonight, she was off men indefinitely. After a few short-lived, disastrous relationships in the early half of her twenties, she'd thrown herself entirely into her business. She would never say she'd sworn them off forever, but she couldn't be bothered until she'd grown this place into something real. Something she could rely on. And then, perhaps, she'd risk the vicissitudes of love again. Not before.

But he didn't seem to share her discomfort around the tone of the conversation. Instead he arched one thick, dark brow, and leaned into it. "Put me to work," he said. "I'll do anything you tell me to, and I won't tell a soul."

Wrist-deep in soft dough, Janey shook her head and smiled.

Chapter Two

Though he didn't mention it to the pretty, curvy woman working beside him, this wasn't Ian's first rodeo as far as kneading bread. As a teenager he'd baked bread nearly every week, packing it up for his school lunches, sharing it with neighbors who inquired. The hobby had brought him great peace through the long, dark afternoons of the rainy English winter. He stayed mostly inside then—baking, reading books about biology—away from the other boys that lived on his street.

He'd sworn the hobby off some time ago, along with several others that involved the baking and eating of sweets. But though it had been years, the movement came back naturally now, the supple material yielding satisfyingly beneath his hands.

The woman, Janey, seemed to notice. "Looks like you do need bread," she joked, and he let out a weak laugh. He wanted to answer, "Not anymore." Not since his parents had put him into the weight-loss program his last year of secondary school. That was all long ago in England, of course. No one here in the states had any idea he'd been such an overweight teenager. So he didn't say a word about it.

"What's your name?" she grunted out as she leaned into her own portion of dough. He was good at this, but she was even better, having already whipped two of the eight loaves the big lump would provide into shape. She moved onto a third as he put his first aside.

"Ian," he offered. "Ian Chisholm." She laughed again, for some reason. She seemed to laugh a lot, and he liked the way it lit up her features. Though it was dark and her hair was hidden beneath her cap, her eyes appeared to be green, and sparked with mischief. He wasn't usually easy in the presence of strangers; a remainder from those days he'd spent locked inside. But he liked how she laughed.

"Ian?" she said. "Is that a requirement, if you're English? To be named Ian?"

"Not at all!" he answered with mock outrage. "Some of us are called Collin, or even Nigel!"

She giggled. "Forgive my ignorance." Her eyes kept floating over to his work, and he pressed his lips together. Though he liked to excel, and in fact he did, especially at work, he wasn't the type who enjoyed assessment or even very much praise.

"You've done this before," she said, right on time.

"Just as a hobby," he improvised. "Never professionally, like you." He arched his brow at her again and smiled, in the way he knew showed off his dimple. Reliably, she blushed and looked back down. The upside of his weight loss was that he had turned out to be rather good looking, or so people told him. He'd found he could leverage that to deflect attention he didn't want, although sometimes it brought him more than he could handle, so it was rather a tradeoff.

When he'd first come to America for grad school he'd careened through several wild situationships, having no idea what he was doing, with women who were drawn by his looks but quickly found his rather sedate, homebody personality to be lacking.

Perhaps if he'd always been seen as good-looking, he reflected. Maybe he'd be used to it by now. Maybe he'd have learned early on to go out and take up space, to accept the accolades and authority people now offered him with little prompting. To go through women as if he had the right, the way they seemed to expect him to. Instead they were almost taken off guard by his interest in their personalities, by his thoughts about the future.

"Fold it over," Janey interrupted his thoughts. "Or it will break along the edge when it rises." He looked down at his loaf. It looked fine to him. He watched the way she rolled her own, stretching it along the top and pressing the edges under in one fluid movement, and tried to copy her.

"Where did you learn to bake?" he inquired.

"Over at the university," she answered. "Culinary arts. What about you?"

He smiled self-consciously that she thought he could bake like her. "Self-taught. Youtube."

She smirked. "Nearly as reliable."

"Oh I don't think so," he teased. "I clearly never learned to make a tight *skin*."

She rolled her eyes.

"I learned as a child," he said carefully as they rolled and kneaded. "As a teenager. It was one of my favorite hobbies." There was no harm in divulging this much, especially with someone who had an affinity for baking. "I made all the bread for my school lunches, and even sold a few loaves in my neighborhood."

"So you are a baker!" she crowed. "Fate sent you to me in my time of need."

He laughed. "It was all very much under the table."

"I see. So what do you study now?"

"Study? I teach!" He pretended offense, though he had only finished graduate school a few years earlier.

She eyed him as she rolled her dough. "Well, what am I supposed to think, with your long scarf?" Her eyes went up. "And shaggy hair?"

"The tweed jacket is supposed to be the giveaway," he deadpanned. "They don't let you buy them without a PhD and a tenure-track post."

"Ah." She nodded, still smiling. "I've seen them at the special shops, under glass. I suppose the elbow patches cost extra?"

He nodded seriously. "Oh, yes. You have to earn them like merit badges."

Her eyes crinkled up again, and a warm feeling spread in his gut. It was never this easy to talk with people. Was she faking it? Sometimes women laughed at every word he said, if they wanted to get into his pants. But she'd made no gesture in that direction. It had been clear since he'd stumbled into the shop that he was mostly a nuisance to her. She was clearly only letting him help now because she needed it.

"There now," she said, looking first at her nine loaves and then at his four. "Not bad, actually, Ian."

"Oh yes? Do you think the skin is tight enough?"

She shot him a look from under her eyelids, and he felt the blood tingle in his palms. Such an odd thing, to be drawn to a woman he'd met only an hour ago. She began covering the dough with plastic wrap.

He glanced over at the dark oven. "Do you think it will be warm enough for the dough to rise?"

Janey followed his gaze, then turned toward the front, where fat flakes of snow could still be glimpsed falling in their lazy circles. She seemed to shiver, although the bakery wasn't cold yet.

"It should hold for now," she said, but he thought he detected a slight hint of anxiety in her voice. Still, she turned to him, catching him with the full force of those intelligent, possibly-green eyes. "Well, we have at least two hours to wait on those. I'll need to get started on those cakes next. Do you want something to eat, since you're stuck here?"

Ian felt his shoulders tense. The truth was, he was hungry. He'd purposefully eaten little today in anticipation of the work party tonight. That was part of his stress about it—social occasions involving food were always difficult to navigate. Either he kept himself back from what he wanted to eat and spent the night miserable, or he overate himself and went to bed with a painful stomach. It was difficult to walk the line he had to walk at someone else's party.

"Oh, I'm all right," he pushed out. "I have a protein bar in my bag."

Janey wrinkled her nose. "A protein bar?" She sounded genuinely offended, and it almost got his back up. Some people, including his old trainers, made his food all their business in order to make sure he wasn't eating too much. Others, including some of his most well-meaning friends, were always trying to get him to eat food he didn't want.

"It'll be fine," he said curtly. "It's all I need." Even as he said it a rumble ripped out of his gut and nearly echoed around the silent, dark room. God. What was it about snow that made everything so silent?

He peered through one eye at Janey, waiting for her nose, wrinkled with surprise, to wrinkle further into scorn.

Instead, she let out a tinkling laugh and shrugged. "Suit yourself," she said, and walked over to the nearby counter. There she reached into a basket and pulled out what looked like an unfrosted, day-old cinnamon roll. Tearing off a piece, she popped it into her mouth. "But if you'd like to keep your energy up, you're welcome to leftovers."

Ian sighed with relief. She wouldn't hassle him, after all. He pulled the protein bar out of his bag, and while it was no doubt dry and mealy in comparison with anything she had on offer here, it did the trick of filling his belly and taming his inner rumbles, at least for the moment.

"Coffee?" she offered when she finished her roll, going to a machine that had a full pitcher on it. "Getting cold now," she said, peering inside dejectedly. "But it ought to do its job."

"That I will have," he offered. He was nowhere near tired, but the power gave no sign of coming back on. With all those cakes on the shelf, it might be quite a late night.

"Milk?" Janey asked, pulling a carton out of the silent refrigerator and frowning at it. She gave it a big sniff. "Not sour yet, at least."

Still, Ian shook his head. "No thanks."

Janey put it back in the refrigerator. "I'd take it out and put it in the snow if we could get out the door." She walked to the front of the store and stood before the windows. Ian trailed her, tracking her gaze outside as she sipped her own milky coffee. A little worried line appeared on her forehead. It looked bright outside now, rather than pitch black, though it was only the reflection of the faintest light from the sky on the snow.

"Any idea when they might get around to fixing the power?" he asked, sipping his bitter, tepid coffee.

Janey shrugged. "It depends on how many outages there are. It could come on in fifteen minutes. It could come on in three days."

Ian shivered. That had happened before. Snow was so rare here on the west coast of Oregon, the cities weren't prepared for it. Even a mild snowfall could cause outages, break trees, and shut down freeways. Sometimes the government had to ship in snowplows all the way from Idaho.

"You'd think they'd store just a little bit of salt down at city hall," he grumbled, and she chuckled.

"You never told me what you study, Professor Ian."

He shook his head. "Not a professor yet. Soon, hopefully. Try not to be too impressed, but I'm the leading expert in the Pacific Northwest on a certain species of Amazonian newt."

Janey slowly, sedately, lifted her coffee to her lips, without looking at him. "Ah. Newts."

He huffed out a laugh. "Yes indeed. They're common here in Oregon, you know, albeit different species than my specialty. They're also common where I grew up in England. I used to collect them on rainy days." He took a sip of coffee. "I wouldn't have dreamed then that I'd end up in a part of America so like where I grew up. Even the rocky coast and rough seas remind me of it, sometimes."

She looked up at him. "Are you homesick?"

Bah. There he went. Getting personal again. But he couldn't help it. Maybe it was the holidays making him think of his home, a little town in the southwest of England. Certainly the boys at school were tossers, but he did sometimes miss the little rows of colorful houses down near the sea, the fish and chip stands, the serene, sunny summers when the tourists flocked south for a taste of a beach...

"No," he said quietly, clearing his throat. "I'm not going back, at any rate. Not for anything more than a brief visit to see my parents. Far too busy at the university. Publish or perish, that's what they say." He was aware his voice had gone low, lower than he wanted it to, and he cleared his throat again.

"And what about you? Did you grow up in Oregon? Did you always know you wanted to be a baker?"

She nodded. "Yes, and yes. My parents live only a few miles from here, on the western edge of town near the forest." A smile touched her lips. "I ran wild in those woods growing up, with all my friends."

He smiled. "And are they still here?"

Janey's smile dimmed a little. "Some," she said. "Most have moved on to greener pastures."

Ian shook his head dubiously. "What could possibly be greener than Corvallis, Oregon?"

Janey laughed, that merry little trill cutting through the gravity of the topic. "Their mistake, isn't it?"

"Quite," he answered, and threw back his last sip of coffee at the same moment Janey downed hers. "Shall we get to it, then?" he said, nodding backward toward the production floor.

"Onward," was all Janey answered, and he followed her back, setting their cups on the coffee machine as they passed.

Chapter Three

"Have you frosted cakes before?" Janey eyed Ian dubiously as she brought three cakes to the kneading board and set them on turntables. He had surprised her with his skill at kneading the bread, but that didn't mean he knew his way around a pastry bag.

"Ah yes, well. I suppose that's a bit different, isn't it? We don't really have this sort of American cake where I'm from."

"Where are you from again?" she inquired suddenly, remembering that Britain was not one large monolith consisting of London, Stonehenge, and probably Scotland.

"It's called Seaton," he said, a note of dismissal in his voice. "It's a small town. We had a bakery though, and you could get a sort of sponge with cream on it. Or a Christmas cake at the holidays."

"That's like a fruitcake?" Janey said, and he nodded. "Ah, I know the one. With fondant rolling down, and the little holly leaves and berries."

He cocked that thick eyebrow again. "That's it."

"But nothing with buttercream? Nothing with a frosting bag?"

He shrugged. "Not in the Seaton bakery."

Janey sighed. He might be pleasant eye candy and a decent conversationalist, but his usefulness apparently had its limit. "I see. Well, I suppose you can wait in the office until the lights turn back on. You can even sleep; there's a sofa in there if you want to try and get comfortable." She eyed his length. He wouldn't fit, but if he didn't mind having his feet stick out off the end it might be all right.

He looked offended. "Sleep? I want to help!"

Janey went from enjoying his company to impatience in nearly the blink of an eye. "I'm sorry! I appreciate your help with the bread, but appearance is everything in these cakes. People special-ordered these for parties and holiday dinners. They're centerpieces. I can't have—" She shook her head in an exaggerated fashion, hoping to bring back the easy, teasing tone of earlier in the evening. "I can't have an amateur working on them!"

He dropped his jaw. "How dare you?"

Janey giggled, relieved. "Believe me, I'm thankful for what you've done. You've saved me at least an hour on getting the rolls on to rise."

"What about this," he said, leaning forward on his elbows on the kneading board. He would get flour on his forearms, but he didn't seem to care. "Why don't I just watch what you do, and maybe I can learn it?"

She shook her head. "You won't be able to do it. Not in one night. Not to the skill level I need."

"Well, I'll be your support then, Rocky Balboa. I'll just stay to the side and massage your back and shoulders when you need it. Splash you with water, things like that."

Janey blinked, trying not to be distracted by the imagined feeling of his hands on her shoulders, rubbing away the knots she knew were there. That she'd allowed to become a permanent feature. She shook her head. There was no time for this nonsense. And deep in her gut she felt it was very unlikely Ian was serious about any of it. She was no wallflower, but men as good-looking as this almost never took notice of her. Ian was just an outrageous flirt. That was all.

"Besides," he pressed. "I'm hardly going to sleep with all that coffee in me."

She shook her head. The man probably lived on coffee. And protein bars. "You're impossible," she said, and tried not to let the grin that lit up his face please her too much.

She turned to the refrigerator, bringing out the bowls of buttercream Angelica had mixed for her that morning. At least those were done. If she were facing the prospect of whipping it all together by hand, she would indeed have had to make eighteen calls in the morning canceling her biggest order of the year. And since the refrigerator was no longer very cold, the frosting was soft and pliable.

"Aren't I just lucky," she whispered to herself.

Ian smiled, and she realized he must have thought she was talking about him. He looked so pleased she didn't correct him, merely turned to get out her spatulas and shaping knives.

"Now, the pattern isn't so complicated," she began explaining to fill the silence, though he hadn't asked about her process. "I want them to look perfect, but I knew ahead of time I'd be doing a lot of them. So I made the design something easy to make and replicate."

"Does that mean I might be able to help?"

"But Ian, it has to look *elegant*."

He met her eyes again. "Am I not *elegant*?"

She shook her head emphatically. "You, sir, are rumpled." She looked him up and down from where he'd perched himself on a stool near the table. His hair was still mashed beneath the hairnet, his sleeves rolled up, his shirt looking lived-in. He'd loosened his top two buttons, which looked rather nice, but much more afterparty than formal dress. She could see the rounded bones of his clavicle just visible on either side. "Which a professor absolutely should be. But nobody wants a rumpled cake."

He looked dejectedly down at his clothing. "But I dressed up for the party."

She laughed. "What do you usually wear?" Admittedly at the beginning of the evening, when he'd first removed the tweed jacket, his white dress shirt and gray trousers had looked rather crisp. They looked far from that now, however.

He shrugged. "What does everyone else around here wear? Flannel."

She chuckled. She did indeed have a dark purple and black check flannel waiting in her locker right now, although she wished she'd brought her little-used down coat instead. She let herself imagine him briefly with his curls loose—a nice English boy dressed casually in jeans, t-shirt, and flannel. It wasn't a bad image, at that.

"I don't suppose biology professors have strict dress codes."

"You should see what the philosophy professors get up to."

Janey snickered, but she was concentrating now. She was attempting to frost three cakes at a time: that was the number of turntables she possessed at this point, although it seemed suddenly wise to invest in more. She carefully covered the first cake with a layer of silky white buttercream, using her widest frosting tip. It took about five spins of the turntable, then she smoothed it out with a clean scraper. Luckily she had an uncountable number of those.

Ian watched, mesmerized, as she repeated the performance on the two other cakes.

"Do you think you can do that?" She couldn't help a little bit of a brag from entering her voice. It was just that he looked so impressed.

"No," he said quickly, then he looked up at the other cakes on the shelves. "If you do it like that, you'll have all of them done in no time."

Janey felt her cheeks pink up with the praise, but she sighed. "The first layer is only the crumb coat." Covering the cakes with a layer of frosting thick and smooth enough to cover every speck of cake, while hiding any crumbs below, all without the benefit of a refrigerator to harden each layer in its place, was going to be the real challenge. And after that the fiddly bits, with careful piping on the sides and sugared cranberries on the top. She wished fervently that Angelica was here.

"I think I may have overcommitted myself," she whispered. She looked up and met Ian's eyes, and they were surprisingly earnest and gentle.

"You can do it, Janey."

She sighed heavily, but she smiled. "Thanks, Coach."

For the next two hours she frosted and piped, while Ian sat on the stool, arms folded. Ordinarily she'd put on loud, fast music to get her through a late night working, or stand-up comedy to make her laugh. But with no power, she needed other distractions.

So she asked him to describe Seaton, and was surprisingly amused by his stories of the seaside, the crashing oceans, the delicious food. It was just as he was describing the summer ice cream season that his stomach ripped another grumble.

She looked up with a laugh, and was surprised to see him looking uncomfortable, and not just out of hunger. "Would you like something?" she asked. "Really. If you don't like rolls, we have plain bread." She didn't know what a man who turned down a cinnamon roll in favor of a protein bar might like to eat. "We're in a bakery, for heaven's sakes. It might be dark and increasingly cold, but you don't have to starve."

He looked around. "Plain bread, eh? Well, it does seem a bit of a waste to be trapped in a bakery and not take advantage."

Janey put down the frosting bag, flexing her gloved fingers which were growing stiff from the careful work. She'd completed almost ten of the cakes in two hours, and her neck and back hurt from stooping. She hated to think she still had six more.

She stripped off the gloves. It was nearly time to do the rolls, anyway. But it wouldn't hurt to take a short snack break.

"What'll you have?" she asked, looking around. "We've got cookies, muffins, some scones."

"Scones?" He pronounced the word with a short 'o', which Janey attributed to his accent.

"Yes, some lovely blueberry scones. They're one of my most popular items. We also have just plain, if you prefer," she said, cutting a quick glance at him. Who knew what he would want? Perhaps blueberries were too indulgent. Or the opposite, if he was really a fitness nut. Weren't they a superfood or something?"

"Can I look at them?"

Janey blinked at him. Was he inspecting them for calories? But the customer was always right, even if he was getting what he wanted late at night, and in the dark. And not paying for it.

"All right," she said evenly, and went to the front, taking a blueberry and a plain scone from the box under the counter. Angelica had wrapped them in plastic before leaving, set to go out tomorrow as day-olds, sold at half-price.

When she returned and handed him the blueberry one, he peered at the chunky, triangular pastry in the dim candlelight as if it were some mysterious artifact. "It's so big!"

"Big? It's a perfectly normal size."

"No. A scone is like this." He made a circular shape with his hand, about the size of a round container of mints from the grocery store. "But thick." He held his fingers apart about three inches.

"Oh," Janey said, recognition dawning on her. "You're thinking of a biscuit."

"I certainly am not," he shut her down, but he was laughing. "A biscuit is something else entirely."

Janey rolled her eyes. "You're clearly very confused. Maybe your long trip from England has rattled your brain."

"I emigrated eight years ago!"

"Just try it, why don't you?"

A crooked smile playing on his lips, he pulled the plastic off the blueberry scone. The smell of butter, satisfying and rich, hit Janey's nose. It seemed to hit him too, and he shivered as if something electric ran through him. But he didn't bite into it. He held it as if it were something strange, and maybe dangerous.

"Go on," Janey prompted gently. "It isn't poisoned."

He looked up at her. "No," he murmured. Then he licked his lips and braced himself as if for something difficult, and she was nearly offended again, but she was distracted from the feeling by the look of his full mouth and white teeth as he gently nipped off the narrow end of the scone.

She watched him chew for several seconds, reading his face for a reaction, before she realized it might be weird for her to watch him eat this closely. But before forcing herself to look away she noticed the way he shut his eyes, as if in pain or relief, at the taste.

"Is it all right?" she asked tentatively.

He nodded.

"Is it as good as a scone?" she asked, deliberately pronouncing the 'o' the way he did.

He nodded again, and she watched him swallow. Then he took another bite; a big one.

Janey smiled nervously as she unwrapped her own scone. "See? You were hungry."

"I am hungry," he said as he swallowed. "All the time."

She didn't really understand what he meant; he was probably just joking. Certainly he was thin and fit. She'd just assumed he was one of those people to whom that state came naturally. He wore it so well. And he must work out, for though he was thin she had glimpsed the curve of muscles in his biceps as he'd kneaded the bread. He carried protein bars in his bag.

But she sensed something delicate in his words, just around the edges, so all she said was, softly: "If you're hungry, perhaps you should eat."

By now he'd polished off the last of the scone, and his eyes opened at her words. He looked oddly different now, something sparking in the candlelit depths of his brown eyes. The bashful awkwardness of the academic was gone, and Janey was suddenly very aware of those knobs of collarbone beneath his shirt, the veins in the forearms that were folded against his chest. He still looked hungry, but not, now, for scones.

"Do you know what it's like to be hungry?" he asked suddenly.

She thought about saying something self-deprecating—thought about gesturing to her own body and saying something like, *what do you think?* Or offering a classic old line like *never trust a skinny chef*, with a false smile.

But she didn't.

Instead, she answered honestly. "No," she said, with a touch of defiance. "I'm a baker. I'm good at what I do. Hunger doesn't factor in."

"Good on you," he said, and his tone was genuinely admiring. "Good on you."

She shrugged. "Sometimes a scone is just a scone." She pronounced it her own way now.

He nodded, his eyes on her face, then cocked his head to the side. "Janey?" he said, stepping toward her.

Involuntarily she moved back, bracing herself with both hands against the kneading board. "What?" she said, alarmed.

"You have...a crumb." Reaching out, he brushed something from her lips with his thumb.

She blinked. He stood close now, eyes intense, his face mere inches away. Where had the quiet man who'd sat on the stool and told her all about his English village gone? Was all this due to the scone? She was familiar with sugar rushes, but she'd never seen someone react this way.

He'd discarded his glasses at some point early in the evening, insisting he only needed them for reading small words in texts and blocking the blue light from his laptop, and now she was unspared the full force of his deep brown eyes. Would he kiss her, over this? Over a scone? Her mental wires crossing between her thoughts and the pastry she'd just eaten, she licked her lips like a cat. It had been a long time since she'd been kissed.

And though he was standing right before her, though he'd given her every warning in body language, somehow when he put his lips on hers it was still a surprise. How could this be happening? Now, in her very own bakery, with a strange man she'd met only hours before? Now, when she had a deadline? Perhaps she'd fallen asleep on the kneading board, collapsed with dough for a pillow, and was dreaming.

But she wouldn't have dreamed this: this man with his gentle hands and hard chest. She put her palms on him and could feel him, muscle and bone, beneath his white shirt. He leaned into her touch. He'd kissed her boldly, but once the connection was made he moved slowly, a caress of lips on lips until she grew almost impatient. *Come now, very hot man*, she wanted to say. *If you're going to kiss me against my own kneading board, do it properly.*

It seemed he read her mind, for he tipped her slightly backwards, deepening the kiss until his tongue swept gently over her lower lip. His hands eased down her body, lingering at her curves, until they found the width of her hips. He gripped her closer to him, then slid both hands down to her bottom.

Do you mind? she shouted mentally, but she couldn't say it aloud now, and anyway it wasn't a protest. It was more a crow of glee. At her size she was rather accustomed to being overlooked by many men, especially those whose self-identity and status were tied to their own fitness. But it certainly wasn't unheard of, no—fit men who liked a woman with substance. It was just her luck to meet one here, tonight, during a power outage she was beginning to think must have been sent by fate itself.

She looped an arm around his neck, and let him hoist her up onto the kneading board. Health and safety be damned, she supposed, although at least the cakes were drying on the countertop, out of range of anything that might happen here on the table.

Though his kiss was becoming hungrier still, she felt it stutter for a moment as one of his hands found its way to her chest. He pulled back slightly, looking at her, ascertaining permission. Putting both hands on his cheeks, she pulled him back in, and he cupped her boldly then with one hand, until she spilled out between his fingers and stopped the kiss herself, gasping from the sensation.

"Ian," she said, trailing her own hand down his chest as she caught her breath. He was muscle and bone, hard and, presumably, beautiful beneath his shirt. But as she searched him she found, just around the side of his hip and above his belt, a piece of flesh to hold onto. It was soft, and she gripped him instinctively. Love handles, didn't they call them? She would put it to its proper use. She found its twin on the other side, and pulled him close to her, looking up at him for another kiss.

He stopped, however, when she grabbed that piece of flesh. Her face was against his shoulder, and his hovered over the back of her neck, where he'd been depositing soft kisses only moments before going entirely still.

Suddenly, he pulled backwards and away from her.

"What?" was all she could ask, stunned.

He cleared his throat, loudly and oddly, like a proper old English colonel or something. His hands were on his hips, and he was bent slightly at the waist, as if something in his belly pained him. "We shouldn't," he said.

Janey frowned. Hadn't he been the instigator? He'd seemed enthusiastic enough only seconds ago. "Why?"

He cleared his throat again. "Only, isn't that your kneading board?" He adjusted his hairnet, which had come askew in the fray. "Isn't it against health and safety?"

Janey balked. "Health and safe—" She cut herself off. What nonsense was this? Her eyes narrowed. Was this some kind of game? Bring a girl down so you can get in her head? *Or maybe*, a voice cut into her thoughts, *he'd simply changed his mind.* Maybe he'd caught himself kissing her, a chubby girl, in a bakery, and stopped himself before he got carried away. It was one thing for fit and beautiful men to kiss a girl like her privately, in the dark. It was something else entirely for them to take her out on the town and introduce her to his mates.

Not that she'd asked for that. She was far too busy to even think of that. She jumped down off the table abruptly. "Fine," she said. "I have to do the rolls." She felt about seventy-five years old when she said it, as if she was about to whip out some knitting needles and fashion him an afghan.

But this was her job. She was a professional, and far too busy to feel like this, and he didn't want her, and she had rolls to do.

"Janey..." His voice was a whispered plea, but she wouldn't look at him. She wouldn't give him the satisfaction. He was one of those men who toyed with one, who wanted to see how much they could get you to give up, and then plied you with nonsense about how he couldn't possibly be good enough for you, or what you deserved, and someday you'd meet someone really, really special.

He was one of those, and she wished those damned doors would unlock.

"I have a lot to do," she said, her voice higher and more strained than she liked. She shut her eyes, trying hard to channel Grace Kelly. She'd never actually seen a movie with Grace Kelly in it, but she'd heard great things...

"I have a lot to do," she repeated, her voice lower now. "You're welcome to sit in the office while I work, or perhaps in the storefront, if you prefer. You can watch for when the lights come back on." What a silly thing to say. As if his monitoring the lights would impact when they came back on. Everyone in town would realize at once when the lights came back on.

But she wanted him out of this room. She glared at him fiercely until he blinked, his eyes black and unreadable. He looked almost sad, the manipulative bastard. As if a man like Ian Chisholm could feel rejected by a woman like her. As if he wasn't the one who'd stopped them, and she was the villain.

"Please, wait in the storefront?" she said in clipped tones. Her phrasing was a question, but she pointed her hand outward in a gesture meant to be inarguable, like a teacher sending you to the principal's office. He accepted it at last, head drooping like the student he resembled, pulling his glasses out from somewhere and putting them back on. Had they been in his pocket this whole time? He straightened the ridiculous hairnet, tucking his curls back in.

"I understand," was all he said.

She restrained herself from giving a loud, *Ha!* In response. He really seemed to think he was the victim here, or at least want to convince her that he was. Was he always this complicated, she fumed? Couldn't a scone be a scone, a deadline a deadline, and a kiss just that? Further nuance and agony were entirely unnecessary. That was how she lived her life, and it was peaceful, and calm, and she had no desire to change it. Though it had been remarkably, regrettably bereft of kisses before tonight.

Well. That was neither here nor there. When she could no longer see the back of him, she turned toward her loaves of bread, perfectly risen on the countertop.

"Now." She spoke softly to them, pushing the ridiculous whirlpool of feelings she'd nearly tripped into away and out of her mind. "My babies. Let's get this done and dusted."

Chapter Four

Ian hadn't felt this miserable in a long time. What were you supposed to do with women? He always gave either too much or too little, and it was never the right amount. It wasn't as if he had some wealth of experience, despite what people assumed. He'd had one or two good friends that were girls back in school, and he'd have been game for anything with them if they'd looked at him that way. But they never had, and then he'd lost weight and gone to college, and now everyone expected him to know what to do all the time.

He'd been on the right track these last eight years, he concluded bitterly. Focusing mainly on work, taking care of his own self, furthering his career. Let everyone else fight these odd, inexplicable battles of lust and status and domination. He wanted none of it.

A friend, perhaps, though. That might be nice. Nights could get downright lonely in his apartment by the university. But he knew instinctively that none of the women who pursued him would be impressed by his shabby, comfortable couch, his closets of dress shirts with fraying elbows (the elbow patch stereotype existed for good reason), or his shelves of books about obscure South American amphibians.

He shivered. This part of the bakery, with its big windows, was significantly cooler than the work floor. If he was honest with himself, he had to admit he'd never really given any of those women a chance. He'd hardly dated at all since arriving in Oregon; maybe the women here would have been perfectly delighted in his bachelor pad. He'd pre-rejected them, before they could do it to him. He was sorry—he didn't aim to hurt anyone, which was why he'd stopped letting it get far enough to where he could. And he was happy this way. He was peaceful.

Many days he doubted whether romantic love was even real. Few people of his acquaintance formed lasting relationships, and when they did they were based on practical concerns: they shared a child, it made sense to raise it together. They cared for each other and were sleeping together, why not split rent? Was he missing some magical piece that everyone had but him? He'd been shut out of romance at a young age when everyone else was learning it, and now he couldn't find his way around it. Perhaps it was nothing more than a fluttery feeling in the belly, or the loins. A simple mutual attraction. Biology. Everything else was just fluff people made up to amuse themselves, to make themselves and their own relationship the perceived center of the universe.

For if love were really that magical and necessary, why would perfectly innocent people find themselves shut out of it? For superficial reasons? It was just genes, searching for compatible genes to create the strongest possible offspring. Everything else was fairytales.

He blinked slowly, conscious of being very tired. Most of the snow had stopped by now, and the sky almost glowed, although he had no idea where the light came from, for clouds still blotted out the stars, and there were no city lights for them to reflect back. Why had he kissed her like that? This Jane—the most ordinary name—this woman he'd never even met before today.

But he liked her. She made him laugh, and seemed to think he was funny too. He couldn't gauge her level of interest in amphibians yet, but something about this small, scrappy bakery felt relatable, somehow. She loved this place. She'd built it herself. She'd made her life about something important, something outside of herself. You had to admire that.

But it wasn't just admiration of her work ethic that drew him. There was something more: something deeper. He'd kissed her before when she'd satisfied his hunger, or perhaps she'd triggered it. This place was warm, and it smelled good, and it called to a part of him that was empty, that longed to be filled. It wasn't even about food, or not just that.

But there was something about his life as he was living it that was slowly wearing away at him. Counting everything—calories, papers, steps, awards and nominations—striving to be seen, for recognition, for praise and promotion. His life required ironclad, constant self-supervision, and it tired one. It left you feeling thin and stretched, even if you were getting the results you wanted.

The scone had been a delicious opposite: an explosion of butter and white flour on his tongue, with just the right amount of sweetness from the blueberries. A gift: fleeting, maybe, but precious. And that was how she felt to him, too: her curves in place, her eyes snapping and intelligent, warm and abundant and just right, just perfectly herself. He wanted her; he hungered for her, with the empty places in both body and soul.

He shook his head. Utterly ridiculous. The sensible thing to do would be to simply get her phone number. In a few days he would call, and they could get a drink or a coffee. See if there was anything there worth pursuing. Approach this like adults.

What was it about the snowstorm that made this dark bakery feel like the only place alive in the world, as if he and Jane were the only two people in it? If she was Jane, perhaps he was Tarzan, alone in a jungle all their own.

He pricked his ears up, listening to her in the back room. He could hear her moving around, presumably taking loaves of bread off the shelf one at a time to portion them out into rolls. They would require shaping and rolling and re-rising. And what if the oven was still cold after the second rise? What had she said? The bakery was doing well, but she hadn't yet paid off her start-up debts. If she crashed this holiday season she would lose not only money, but future customers, and reputation too. Corvallis was a small town, but there were other bakeries here. People had choices when they ordered their holiday treats.

Abruptly, Ian rose and walked back. "Let me help you, Janey."

She was leaning over the kneading board, a small ball of dough in each gloved hand as she rolled them in circles, making sure the ends were tucked under properly, the skin on top tight.

She stopped and looked up at him, blinking. She didn't send him back to the front immediately, however, and he stood up taller.

"I might be an idiot," he continued, which prompted something from her almost like a surprised laugh. "But there's no sense in your business paying for it. I can roll out bread."

She cocked her head to the side, lips pressing together briefly in an expression that looked a little like regret. But she nodded. "Fine. You're right. I'm sorry I lost my temper."

It was hard to tell in the dim light, but he thought he saw the briefest flush of red on her neck. "We can be adults."

"Yes," he said enthusiastically. "Adults. That's just what I was thinking." It made him oddly hopeful, how she echoed his thoughts. Perhaps she was still open to that other path—that practical, mature path. At the end of the night, so long as there were no other disasters, he would ask for her phone number.

He washed his hands and put on a spare apron, joining her at the kneading board. "How many have you done?" he said as he floured his hands.

"I've finished about thirteen of the two dozen."

"Halfway? Not bad," he said, looking at the countertop where the pale lumps of dough had been transformed into orderly rows of small, perfectly round bread rolls, gently rising into each other like fat little piglets.

Janey let out a big sigh. "Maybe, but everything will hit a wall if we don't get the oven back on."

"Keep the faith," Ian encouraged. But he glanced over at where the oven stood, big and dark in the back wall of the place. "How did they do it in the old days?" he mused. "Can you bake bread over a fire?"

Her mouth quirked up. "Ovens are actually very old, you know. Long before electricity, people were using ovens, powered with wood or coal or whatnot."

Ian nodded. He was aware of this; half the homes in Seaton still held woodfire stoves. "But what about before that?" he pressed, his natural curiosity getting the better of him. "Before they had iron to make stoves with?"

She looked up at him, blinking, and he wondered if she would tease him for being a nerd. The oddest things had always prompted his curiosity. He'd landed on newts, but it could have been space, or dinosaurs. Or apparently the history of the oven.

Janey turned back to her business, but she spoke knowledgeably. "In Ancient Mesopotamia they fashioned ovens out of earth and bricks. They filled them with rocks heated in fires to bake the bread. Perhaps there were ovens even before that, but the Mesopotamians invented bread—and pies—and that's as far back as we can track cooking with wheat meal."

Ian tried not to let his surprise interrupt the delicate motion he was copying from her of rolling the bread into perfect little dough balls with two hands. "Did you learn all that in culinary school?"

He saw her roll her eyes. "Just because I went to culinary school and not phd in newts doesn't mean I'm stupid."

He'd messed up again. "Of course not," he insisted, anxiously aware that insisting too loudly that he didn't think that would make it seem all the more that he did. But just as he was about to become really unhappy, he caught the little smile on her face. She was teasing him again. He released a sigh, half-relief, half-exasperation. "You mustn't frighten me that way, Janey," he said. "You'll hurt my feelings."

It was a tease, a scolding in fun like they'd been doing all evening. But it was also an experiment: a confession, and something like vulnerability. Because it was at least a little bit true.

She looked up, and he wondered how she would respond. Her glowing eyes trailed up his arms as he rolled the dough. "Surely I couldn't frighten a big strong man like yourself," she said slowly. Her words were flirtatious, but her tone was difficult to read.

He smiled, and swallowed, and thought he'd try another experiment while he was at it. "Did you know I used to be very overweight?" His tone was almost avuncular. This was not a conversation he'd ever grown smooth at having, the few times he'd had it at all. Mostly he never told people about it, and they never asked.

"Oh," Janey said, wrinkling her nose. "Like me?"

Ian laughed softly. "No, not like you." His eyes ran appreciatively over her generous figure once more. "You look wonderful. But I was much larger than that."

She looked surprised, and her eyes crawled over him again, in the way they always did when people learned this. He didn't know what they were looking for: where he'd hidden it, maybe? As if he'd drawn it all behind him and held it in place with a large bag clip? Or were they trying to imagine the face they'd previously found handsome with a chin or two more? Would Janey have found him handsome then?

Apparently finished with her inspection, she met his eyes again. "Oh," she said, and turned, transferring her most recent half-dozen bread rolls to the counter.

He sighed. It wasn't a bad reaction. She'd neither congratulated him too heartily on leaving all that behind, or lapsed into apologetic insistence that it didn't matter, that size and weight never mattered. Perhaps she didn't care at all. Perhaps that was the best approach of all.

Encouraged, he pushed further. He'd already apologized for what happened before, but since he'd come this far, he might as well explain. "It's only that when people learn that about me, it sometimes changes how they see me."

She frowned in amusement as she rolled. "Why?"

"I don't know," he said, somewhat defensively. "You think I make the rules?"

She shook her head. "Sorry. I'm not doubting your experience. I'm just wondering why something like that would change a person's perspective on you." She continued rolling, but he could see she was thinking. "Well, I suppose I do know. People must treat you differently now."

"Exactly," he said, relieved she could see it. "That's exactly it. And don't get me wrong, of course I like it."

She arched an eyebrow up at him as she rolled. "Now we're being honest."

He grinned defiantly. "Well, I do. People make way for me in crowds. They assume I'm good at my job because I look the part. People look into my grocery cart in approval and envy rather than judgment." He'd meant the last part to sound like a joke, but it hadn't really come out that way. But Janey was nodding, as if she understood.

"And women react differently, I suppose?"

He nodded slowly. "Of course. Of course they do. But that's it", he said, getting back to his point. He was still trying to apologize. "You see, maybe it's silly to still feel this way after so long. I lost the weight almost a decade ago. But after seeing people's behavior change so dramatically around something so superficial...it's hard for me to trust if they mean it."

Janey nodded, still rolling. She didn't meet his eye, though he felt now like it was on purpose. Was she avoiding his gaze, or just digesting what he'd said?

"So you aren't in the habit of passionately kissing women in their workplaces? And then dropping them almost immediately?"

Ian choked out a little laugh. "No. Particularly not while wearing a hairnet."

Her eyes went up to his hair, a hint of that warm smile reappearing, and the tension in his heart eased. Did she understand?

"We're coming to the end of the rolls," she said suddenly, and he looked down. They had indeed gone through the lot much faster than seemed possible. "You *are* good at this," she said, as though it surprised her, and he knew she was teasing him again.

But when she looked up at the oven in the far wall, her face was forlorn. "We've got only a few hours," she said, glancing back up at the trusty battery-operated clock on the wall. "Then I'll have to start making phone calls that people's orders are canceled." She shut her eyes in exasperation. "If I'm able to charge my phone by then."

Ian pressed his lips together. "I'm sure the outage is city-wide. People will understand."

Janey nodded as she stretched plastic over the hundreds of rolls now waiting on the separate counter. She'd put them as close to the stove as possible, perhaps hoping its final gasp of heat, if any lingered, might help them rise.

"And the cakes look beautiful," Ian added, hoping to banish the forlorn expression from her face. She'd managed to frost the rest of them while he'd been up front, somehow. She was amazing.

"Thank you," she said. "At least there's that." They stood across from each other in the dark room, the kneading table, now empty, stretching between them.

"What now?" he asked. "We've a few hours. Do you want to try and sleep?" He smiled. "I've heard there's a sofa in the back room."

Janey glanced up at him, and then her brows went downward in a little v, puzzling him. "Uh huh," she said. "It's a good idea." She turned toward the back of the bakery, but nodded to him as she did so. "Are you coming?"

Her innocuous question sent a rush of blood through his body. Had she forgiven him, then, for earlier? "Is there room for two?"

"No," she answered simply. "There's barely room for one." She turned to look back at where he lingered by the kneading board, and her eyes flashed to it. "But I can't have you out here. Health and safety."

Again the possibility of double-meaning in her phrase had its impact on his circulatory system. But she had turned away, toward the dark back of the shop. Ian swallowed, put his head down, and followed her.

Chapter Five

She'd had the sofa installed in her office in the early days of the brick and mortar shop, when she worked so late and got up so early to continue that everything had just been easier if Janey spent some of her nights here. As the bakery had gained some self-sustaining momentum in the spring and summer, she'd used it less and less. But was glad she'd kept the sofa around, in case of nights like this one.

She turned to look at Ian as he entered, gazing around at the small space. Apart from the sofa there was a desk with her computer on it and a swivel chair, and little else. The office was small but tidy, and unless the bills were piling up she enjoyed being back here. It was like a little oasis away from the madness the bakery floor could become when Dax and Angelica were busy in the back and customers were flooding the front.

Ian, however, looked less than impressed, and his thick brows knit as he looked over the sofa. "Are we both supposed to sleep on that?"

Janey let herself laugh aloud. His long and lanky form was unlikely to fit on it even alone. "Watch this," she said. Walking up, she reached into the crack between the sofa back and cushions, and pulled. The secret mattress opened easily, and though it filled the whole room, there was just enough space to make it into a bed.

Ian made a low whistle. "Clever."

Janey smiled again, and gestured at it. Gamely he came and sat on its edge, but when she didn't move, he didn't lie down.

"Aren't you coming?" he said casually, almost as if they were an old married couple. As if sharing a bed when practical circumstances demanded it were obvious, and no big deal. Maybe that's just the sort of man he was: practical. Janey remembered how he'd put his wounded ego aside and insisted on helping her with the bread, just because that was clearly the right thing to do.

Maybe she'd misjudged him from the start. She'd thought he was high-maintenance, a player of games; or just a player. But what he'd told her about himself gave her new insight, and some relief. She hadn't liked to think of him as cruel or shallow. In fact there were a variety of ways she preferred to think of him, and found he fit them even better now that she understood, at least a little, where some of his hesitation came from.

"I don't think I could sleep now if I wanted to," she said, a coil of stress streaking through her belly as she again thought of the rolls on the countertop. "Too much coffee."

"Ah," he said. "Me as well, actually. Come and sit anyway." He patted the bed beside him, and she smiled. Whatever lapse in confidence he'd had, he seemed to have weathered it. "At least have a rest, if you can't sleep."

So she sat, and as she did, she couldn't help it. She let her thigh slide up to his. "There isn't much room in here," she said by way of apology or explanation, and he laughed a throaty laugh.

"No."

She let her eyes wander to his lap, where his hands were clasped together. They were rather nice hands, with well-shaped knuckles—pale, and with a light threading of fine dark hairs. His thighs echoed their shape: well-muscled, tapering into the hard bulge of his knee. She remembered the round edge of his collarbones she'd glimpsed through his shirt earlier, and turned to see. They were still there, peeking out of the edges of his dress shirt. He was lovely, but sometimes he seemed all muscles and hard bones. For the first time she realized he'd pulled away from her the moment she'd found a soft spot, on his back, just above his hip.

"How did you lose all the weight?" she asked. She was mildly curious, having attempted a variety of diets herself that had brought cupfuls of misery alongside mere spoonfuls of success. But she didn't really ask the question for herself. The last conversation she wanted to have right now was about calories and portion control. If wishes were horses she might have wished herself thinner, just to access the kind of privileges and respect he'd mentioned earlier. But she'd found an equilibrium in her life, and she was happy with her body as it was.

She wasn't curious about diets. But she was curious about him, and the gap that apparently stretched between the face he showed the world and the mind that had unruly appetites of all kinds.

He cleared his throat. "Fat camp, I think you call it, here in the states. It doesn't work for everyone, not in a lasting way. But it worked for me. My parents sent me at the end of secondary school, and maybe I was just motivated enough…just miserable enough…and perhaps young enough, too, that I was able to absorb the habits they were trying to teach. They became a normal part of my life, to where it would be difficult, now, to switch back."

Janey was surprised by the melancholy in his tone. "Would you want to?" The majority of diets failed, she knew, and most people who wanted to lose weight would think him very lucky.

Ian shook his head. "No. But it was hard, Jane. Can I tell you?" The final phrase was casual, rhetorical. But she sensed it was novel for him to tell anyone, and she nodded quietly. "It took a lot out of me." He spread his arms. "Literally!"

Janey smiled.

"And there were surgeries, and pills, and so much hunger." He shook his head. "There are times I wonder if it was quite worth it."

"But you said you're happier now, with how the world treats you?"

He smiled. "Yes, that's undoubtedly true." He looked at her, his eyes temporarily mocking. "I doubt you'd be sitting so close to me if I was a fat man with a PhD in newts."

Janey was oddly miffed by his comment. "Have I given any indication that I would like you less if you were fat?"

He blinked, and she could see him processing that she'd said aloud that she liked him. Well, that part should have been obvious by now. Annoyed, and also bold because she was annoyed, she reached out a hand and put it on his flat stomach. "You think if this were softer, I would want to kiss you less?" Boldness turning to brazenness, and not wanting him to speak or argue with her, she leaned up and planted a kiss on his lips.

They were familiar from before, though now they were frozen with surprise. Was she moving too fast? Well, this whole thing was too fast. That didn't mean she couldn't embrace it. And true, he'd cut her off before, but that was before he'd told her about his past. He'd seemed to want her just fine before she'd touched his soft places. Now that she knew better where to tread. She softened her lips, leaving her hand on his belly. It was muscled, but soft in the way that a boneless, unprotected place can be. His lips slowly unfroze, parting softly against hers. Emboldened, Janey sat up and swung a leg over his lap until she was straddling him, kneeling over him. A soft moan came from him, against her mouth.

"Do you want me to stop?" she asked carefully. How deep did this go, this hesitation? These fears? Everyone had scars from highschool of one kind or another. Were his bad enough still, in this accomplished adult man, to stop him now? She stopped kissing him, and pulled back.

They were not. He put his palms on her thighs and pulled her over him, until she could feel him hard against her. It was as if he'd taken her question as a challenge; she hadn't offered it in that spirit, but if that was what he wanted, well. She was up for it. She ran her hands over his pectorals and around his neck, seeking balance as he put one long hand in the small of her back and the other around the back of her neck. He was tall, but their position made it so her face was above his, and with his kiss he pressed up into her, offering her the tip of his tongue as she angled down onto him With his lower body he did the same, positioning her over him until gravity forced them to grind together, and the feel of him through both of their clothes made her shudder.

He kissed her that way for some time, suspended over him, grinding against her through the barrier of their clothing, until her breath began to come in short gasps. "Now, Ian," she said, and felt his skin prickle under her call. "Before it's too late."

"You're sure?" he asked, his own voice breathless. "We can just do this for now, if you like."

She liked the sound of that 'for now', as if there might be other times. Other times they could pursue other things, back here on the mattress, or maybe somewhere else. She had a sudden vision of him meeting her roommates, meeting Dax and Angelica, how her friends would eye each other knowingly, because Janey finally had a man. She saw the two of them standing together in some unknown kitchen—Ian's, in her fantasy—cooking dinner together. Something healthy and real and filling, that would satisfy them both. Watching silly movies together, eating popcorn, then doing this and other things in the privacy of a shared bedroom.

"No," she insisted, bringing herself back to the present. All that was for another day. All that may or may not happen, but for now, she wanted this. "I want you, Ian," she said, gripping him around the neck and fixing his eyes with her own.

He nodded, and as she trailed a hand down his chest, popping open the remaining buttons of his dress shirt, he slid a hand beneath the waistband of her jeans. With a little help from her he slid them off, letting them fall to the floor. Helping him along, she pulled off her shirt, undershirt, and bra in one movement, dropping them to the side.

She hovered over him completely nude now, and if she were to confess it, she rather liked this configuration. Him, still half-clad in his professional suit. Her, entirely nude, as if he'd ordered her from an agency. She felt like a very bad girl, in the best of ways.

The inequity didn't last for long, however. In a moment he had shed the shirt, and then the trousers and the boxers beneath them, and she thought he might lay her out on the bed, stretching beside her to continue their kiss. But the mattress was too short for him, she could see, even fully extended, and he kept her sitting in his lap as he put his mouth to her bare breasts.

She closed her eyes, savoring the feel of him, the warm and gentle touch. She admired what she could see of him too, liking this view. Whatever it had cost him, he had clearly worked very hard indeed, and was beautifully sculpted. She ran a hand along the soft skin of his back, the curves of his muscled shoulders, the bumps of his long spine. She wiggled, and he let her slide down until their faces were even again. Holding his eyes in hers, she slipped a hand around behind, finding that soft place on his back again, putting her palm to it. It was nothing, really. A bit of skin. The slightest amount of energy, stored for future use. It was healthy. That was how bodies worked.

To her great relief he didn't pull away now. Instead he lifted her—easily, with his strong arms—until she was angled above him again. This time there were no clothes between them, and when gravity brought them together, there was no pressure at all. Only a slipping downward, like pulling a glove onto a hand, as she sat upon him and took him into herself.

His mouth parted a little when she did, and she felt why. His fit was tight and hot, and because she sat on top the rhythm was up to her. He held her, his fingers splayed out on the flesh of her bottom, keeping still, his eyes shut as if concentrating.

The room was quiet, apart from the sound of their stolen breaths. It had been a long time since she'd done this, but it was impossible to forget, and she moved until he stroked just the right places in her, toward the front, again and again. She could feel the tension building in him as he kept himself still, and she could see he was deliberately giving this to her, putting her in charge of it, until the last possible moment when his fingers grew desperate in her flesh.

He gripped her then, rolling them both onto the mattress until she was beneath him, weaving their fingers together and lifting her arms until the backs of her hands were on the mattress as he took over the rhythm and pressed himself into her, hard and shuddering. She felt herself give beneath him, warm and weighed down while the feeling radiated from her center to her toes and fingertips.

"Oh God," she said, as she ran her nails over his damp back. "Oh God, Ian."

He was quiet, his face hidden in her neck, but his thumb stroked her cheek as he drew deep, ragged breaths.

Janey sucked in a breath herself, wanting to speak, to say something. That was great, she wanted to say. But though their chemistry truly had surprised her, that seemed too mundane. As if she were the English stereotype: *jolly good show*! But just as she opened her mouth to try to express her profound enjoyment, the world around them whooshed to life.

Everything turned on so quickly it was almost impossible to imagine the whole bakery—the whole world, it had felt—had been pitch black only seconds before. The lights in the office flicked on. Light flooded in from the production floor through the gap in the door. The computer next to her sucked in a breath of life, and she heard the beep-beep of her phone announcing that it was finally being charged.

Best of all, she heard an enormous rushing sound from the other side of the nearest wall, and she knew that the oven had roared to life.

"My buns!" she called out joyfully, and she rolled a stunned Ian to the side. Grabbing her clothes from the floor she darted to the restroom, washing and dressing, and in moments she reemerged, freshly scrubbed, her baker's hat perfectly placed, snapping on her gloves.

Ian, shyness evaporated, stood naked and stunned in the door of the office. She took a moment to admire the tall drink of water of a man that he was. But she forced herself to look away. "Put on your clothes!" she instructed merrily. "Health and safety! Besides, I can't have you distracting me now!"

A faint but earnest smile crossed his face, and he turned. After a few minutes he too emerged from the office, clothed now, and went to the bathroom to wash. When he came out, he grabbed a disposable hairnet from the box.

"What can I do?" he said, and she pointed him in the direction of the pastry brush and egg wash.

Chapter Six

Though the buns were slow to mix and slow to rise, they were quick to bake, and Ian admired the way they popped quickly out of the oven, forming neat rows of golden, steaming rolls from what had been soft, raw dough. Janey let them cool as long as she could, explaining that if they were bagged up too soon the steam would make them soggy.

Ian admired her as she worked, quick and professional, putting everything in its right place. It wasn't Amazonian newts, but he was reminded of the satisfaction he'd found in baking bread when he was young.

He did the jobs she gave him, appreciating that she explained what they were for. They worked steadily, and it wasn't until a few hours had passed and all the rolls were bagged up and all the cakes boxed and in the massive industrial refrigerator, that he remembered it might be worthwhile to go outside and fetch his phone from his car.

He felt inexplicably reluctant to pass through the doors, though there was nothing that said he couldn't just come right back in. It was Christmas Eve, and there were no classes to teach. Most professors would have canceled anyway after a night like that, if the power was on at the university at all.

Well, it didn't matter. He'd just pop out and get the phone and come back in, keeping Janey company until the other bakers got here.

"When are they meant to come in?" he asked, glancing at the clock on the wall. It was quarter to six.

"In fifteen minutes," Janey said, and he thought he caught, satisfyingly, the same sort of regret in her face that he was wrestling with.

"I'll be right back," he said, somewhat apologetic, and she nodded, trailing him around the barrier to the front of the store.

When he looked at the big bay windows, however, he was shocked to see a line of people extending out into the snow. Underdressed Oregonians, lacking down coats and proper footwear for snow, stood gripping themselves in the cold, teeth gritted, waiting.

"Are these people all here for rolls?" he asked, but when he turned to Janey she looked just as surprised.

"I only took twenty-six orders," she said. "And the cake pickups are spread throughout the day." The line of people was far more than that, and when the ones in the front spotted them behind the counter, their faces lit up. They began waving and speaking words that neither Ian nor Janey could hear from behind the glass.

"What are they saying?" Janey asked, trying to make it out. "Their stoves all went out, and they're hungry?"

"They want bread," Ian said, with a shrug. "And muffins. And cookies. And scones."

"Proper scones," she teased, wonder still on her face. "Or the American kind?"

Ian licked his lips. "Whatever you have, I should think."

Janey looked up at him, her face a mixture of pride and apprehension. "I think I'm going to need some help, even after Angelica and Dax arrive. Will you stay with me today?"

Ian nodded. "I'll stay with you. As long as it takes."

Janey sighed in relief, took his fingers and squeezed them, and went to unlock the door.

Get the News with AM LaMonte's newsletter...

Do you like cozy, laugh-out-loud romantic comedies with a lot of heart? How about epic, heart-pounding historical romance? For all the latest information on freebies, promotions, and upcoming releases, subscribe to my newsletter at:

substack.com/@amlamonte

Leave a review?

Did you know reviews are one of the most powerful tools an author has for getting their books out into the world? Honest reviews bring in new readers and help spread the word! If you enjoyed the book, consider leaving a review on its Amazon or Goodreads listing. You can write as much or as little as you like, or even just drop some stars. I'd be so grateful!

More books by this author available on Amazon and KU!

Trick of the Light: A Delectable Ghostly Romance

When city girl Tessa Smythe blows into rural Greyview, Oregon, fresh out of a bad relationship and newly unemployed, she is determined to win the baking contest she signed up for weeks ago. She is determined to win, despite knowing nothing about baking and not particularly caring for sweets. But when she nearly burns her short-stay apartment to the ground with her first batch of chocolate chip cookies, she realizes she is in dire need of help.

What she didn't expect, however, is for that help to come in the form of the ghost of a grumpy baker named Walter who died in 1962. Despite her fear, Tessa makes an agreement with the astonishing phenomenon: if he can help her learn to bake and win the contest, she will help him resolve his unfinished business and pass over to the other side.

But can Tessa really learn to bake like a professional in only four weeks? And what if Walter discovers his unfinished business lies not in his past life, but in the present, right here with Tessa?

Keep My Candle Bright: A Love Story From the Gilded Age

In the opulence and turmoil of Gilded Age Manhattan, the young and ambitious Helen Riddell dreams of being a journalist. When she slips out of her domineering father's house to document conditions in Five Points—the city's most notorious slum—she meets Rafe "Mack" Macleod, a Scottish immigrant and sex worker who captures her heart. From riotous turn-of-the-century New York to the light and art of Belle Epoch Paris, Rafe and Helen must test their powerful connection against uncompromising class divisions, sexist institutions, and vindictive exes bent on avenging unrequited debts.

And coming soon on February 7!

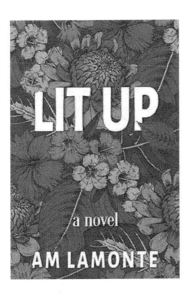

Lit Up: A Small Town Romance in the Foggy Woods

Valentine Sherwood is trapped. For years she's been working the same job at a shabby diner, while her friends moved on and the town shrank around her. When a mysterious troublemaker with an eyepatch and a checkered past comes to town, he offers her a game: come up with a series of dares for each other to get them to take risks, leave routine behind, and ultimately change their lives for the better. But can Valentine find the courage to take a risk after so many years of playing it safe? And what if what she's risking is her own heart?

About the author

Located in Central California, AM LaMonte loves to backpack and travel. An ex-gifted kid, she's worn a lot of hats and worked a lot of jobs like cashier, preschool teacher, and baker, and volunteered as an all-important kitty- and guinea pig-petter at her local Humane Society. Now she reads and writes extensively while caring for three small humans, two guinea pigs, and numerous plants.